# SONNY'S
## Little Adventures

By Lee Cutchall

**Sonny's Little Adventures**

iUniverse books may be ordered through booksellers or by contacting:

iUniverse
1663 Liberty Drive
Bloomington, IN 47403
www.iuniverse.com
844-349-9409

Because of the dynamic nature of the Internet, any web addresses or links contained in this book may have changed since publication and may no longer be valid. The views expressed in this work are solely those of the author and do not necessarily reflect the views of the publisher, and the publisher hereby disclaims any responsibility for them.

Any people depicted in stock imagery provided by Getty Images are models, and such images are being used for illustrative purposes only.
Certain stock imagery © Getty Images.

ISBN: 978-1-6632-6159-5 (sc)
978-1-6632-6160-1 (hc)
978-1-6632-6158-8 (e)

Library of Congress Control Number: 2024906112

Print information available on the last page.

iUniverse rev. date:  03/21/2024

**Hi,** my name is Sonny.
Thanks for coming with me to find big adventures!

Hmmmm... Where should we start?

Oh, I know!!!

Why don't we start with my first memories... let's see. I remember being warm and cozy, maybe a bit crowded but that was ok, I was soooo comfortable. I don't think I opened my eyes for days, but when I did,

OH BOY the things I saw!!

Apparently, I had a little sister and a big brother. They were warm and soft like me.

It was a lot of fun playing with them and getting to know them.

There was Georgie, he was the biggest and he made sure that everyone knew it. When it came time for breakfast, I had to get there before Georgie or there would be nothing left.

He would growl and push me back.

I first thought Georgie was just mean, but then I realized what he was doing. He was making sure little Amy got to eat first. You see, she was so small and my big brother, Georgie, knew that she needed his help.

That was my first lesson: Try to help someone when you can.

Ever since then, I have always looked up to Georgie.

He became my first hero because he made it his job to protect our little sister.

My sister, Amy, was so gentle. She was so kind and she always, always listened to me. She had a way of just looking at me and making me feel like the most important pup in the world.

I could talk to her about anything. We would spend hours walking and talking about the things we saw and the way we felt.

And let me tell you about my mom.

She was so smart, and she always made it her job to take care of me, and Amy, and Georgie. Although, she would scold us when we got to playing too rough, we all knew that she loved us so much and would do anything and everything to keep us safe. Georgie and I would not make that easy for her. It seemed like we were always getting into trouble.

I remember finding the door open one time and I could not resist, I had to go exploring, looking for my big adventure.

Down the steps I ran, and straight into the road. I had never been in the road before, and I could not believe how scary it was seeing the cars coming toward me.

And then, all of a sudden, I felt like someone knocked me down. Then, everything went dark.

I hurt all over.

What have I done?!

I knew I was not supposed to go out that door, now I was hurt, but the next thing I knew my mom grabbed me by the back of my neck and carried me back into the house.

For just a moment, mom scolded me for going outside but then she started licking me all over and checking everything, making sure that I was ok.

That sure was a scary little adventure.

I sure got lucky this time and that was another big lesson for me to learn:

Listen to mom, she is always trying to keep me safe.

One day, there were new people in our house.

They seemed very nice. They were playing with us and scratching mom on top of her head. I could not understand what they were saying, but I wasn't scared. There was a really tall lady called mom by a cute little girl named Isabella.

Isabella and I were playing so hard I did not even notice when they took me out of the house and into their car and we drove away.

I kept looking back wondering about Amy and Georgie and my mom.

When I realized they were left behind, I was so sad and started to whine a little bit, but then I remembered how much mom took care of us and how much Georgie watched over Amy and that made me feel better.

That was the last time I saw them, but they will always be a part of my little adventure.

My new house.

Isabella was just amazing. She would play with me and talk to me and rub my belly. She was so nice, and she made me feel so happy.

I always missed my mom and Georgie and Amy, but I knew I would be ok with Isabella as my new sister.

So, Isabella and I started looking for our big adventures together.

One morning really early, I woke up to Isabella screaming.

It scared me so much, but then I saw that she was not screaming because she was hurt or scared but she was screaming because she was so happy.

I didn't know what in the world was going on, but I knew that Isabella was excited and happy: SO I WAS TOO.

Isabella got dressed so fast, grabbed me up into her arms, and ran out the door. Everything was so bright and new! The whole yard was white and cold and before I could do anything Isabella set me down on the ground that was covered in white fluffy snow.

SNOW!!!

OH, MY GOODNESS!! I LOVE SNOW! It felt amazing under my feet and running through the piles of snow was so much fun, I would push my nose deep in the snow and run like a crazy dog. Isabella and I would play for hours and hours, chasing each other in the snow. She would throw snowballs at me, and I would try to catch them and eat them.

It turned out that snow days were some of the best little adventures a puppy could have.

One warm morning, when the snow had been long gone, Isabella woke me up and I watched as she stuffed a lot of things in her bags. I didn't know where she was going but I sure hoped I got to go too.

As it turned out, we were going on a camping trip, just Isabella, her mom and me. When I found out where we were going, I just KNEW this was going to be my BIG adventure.

After a quick ride, they were working on setting up a tent in the middle of the forest and I was running around exploring everything. That first trip to the forest was amazing. I saw things I had never even thought about before. I saw a squirrel jumping from tree to tree in the air, just like a bird! I saw water rushing by in a creek and over rocks and I found a little turtle. He looked so crazy, nothing like anything I had ever seen before. His back was hard and cold and when I got close enough to sniff, his head would disappear, but after a moment he would stick his little head and feet out and just walk away.

That night Isabella and her mom got into the tent and went to sleep but I stayed just outside the tent by the door.

I know I probably slept a little bit, but mostly I was trying to stay awake to make sure they were safe. I remember thinking as I lay there in front of that tent that Georgie would be proud of me for taking care of my family.

Boy that camping trip was the best little adventure.

OK, so I have had some pretty cool little adventures, but I am still waiting for my BIG adventure. I heard Isabella and her mom talking about going on a boat ride. I didn't even know what a boat was, but I was hoping this would be my chance for a big adventure.

We all got in the car, and we drove for what seemed like forever until we got to a place that smelled SO strange. I could even taste salt in the air.

IT WAS WONDERFUL!

I jumped out of the car and ran around everywhere. There were so many huge birds. There were even birds that had GIGANTIC mouths. Isabella called them Pelicans. I never imagined there could be such strange and noisy birds.

Isabella carried me onto this huge boat, there were lots and lots of people and everyone just loved me. Those strangers would scratch me on the top of my head and run their fingers down my back. I was having so much fun.

Then the big boat started to move, and I just panicked a little bit and started barking at everything! Everyone was laughing at me and somehow that calmed me down, so I knew everything would be OK.

As that big boat carried us out into the ocean and things calmed down, I remember sitting in Isabella's lap. She and I were just looking out across the water. It was very peaceful, and I knew that I was the luckiest puppy around.

That was a beautiful little adventure.

One afternoon, I came bouncing into the bedroom with my favorite toy, only to find Isabella sitting on her bed crying. I didn't understand what was wrong and I do not think I had ever seen her cry before, but I did not like it, it made me very, very sad.

I gently placed my toy in her lap and then I sat next to her and leaned against her shoulder. As Isabella sat there, she had tears rolling down her face. It made me so sad, and I did not know what to do to help her. So, I just sat there leaning against her, and she gently hugged me. Then hugged me tighter and tighter.

27

That was just about the saddest time in my life; to watch Isabella cry like that. I stayed with her for a long time until she stopped crying and she just talked and talked to me. I didn't know what she was saying but I think it made her feel better having me there. That made me feel needed.

It was a sad, but wonderful little adventure for me.

28

One cool, spring morning, I was awakened by an unfamiliar smell. It made my mouth water and my tummy growl. What in the world was it??

As I ran down the stairs to the kitchen, I saw Isabella and her mom laughing and having fun. There were so many new smells, I just didn't know what to do. Then, they opened the door to the oven and there was the most wonderful smell, along with a blast of hot air.

That was my first little adventure with PEANUT BUTTER COOKIES!

Oh, my goodness, I just couldn't believe how they tasted. I never knew anything could taste that good.

As we all sat there, eating those peanut butter cookies, I realized this was a great little adventure, too.

29

That night, Isabella and her mom were laughing and talking. They did such strange things in the living room. They put pillows and blankets everywhere. They even made a big tent with a blanket hanging from the ceiling fan!

It reminded me of our camping trip, and I was so glad to see them happy.

As they lay on the floor next to each other and drifted off to sleep, I sat on the couch looking down at them and I thought,

"I have spent so much time looking for my big adventure, but I discovered that all my little adventures made up my LIFE."

And THAT is my BIG ADVENTURE.

**THE END**

... OR just the beginning. 😊

Printed in the United States
by Baker & Taylor Publisher Services